The Vanishing

The
Vanishing

TIM KRABBÉ

Translated from the Dutch by
Claire Nicolas White

RANDOM HOUSE   NEW YORK

This work was originally published in Dutch, as *Het Gouden Ei* (*The Golden
Egg*), by Uitgeverij Bert Bakker, Amsterdam, in 1984. Copyright © 1984 by
Tim Krabbé.

The publication of this book was made possible by a grant from the
Foundation for the Production and Translation of Dutch Literature.

Library of Congress Cataloging-in-Publication Data
Krabbé, Tim.
   [Gouden ei. English]
   The vanishing / by Tim Krabbé : translated from Dutch by Claire
Nicolas White.
      p. cm.
   ISBN 0-679-41973-X
   I. Title.
PT5881.21.R26G6813 1992
839.3'1364—dc20   92-56826

Manufactured in the United States of America
98765432
First U.S. Edition

The Vanishing

1

Smooth as spaceships, the cars full of tourists moved south down the long, wide turnpike. Evening fell over the wavy landscape bordering the Autoroute du Soleil and turned it violet; the ribbon of cars was thinning out. Rex Hofman and Saskia Ehlvest had been on the road for ten hours now and were still about an hour's drive from their first night's destination: a hotel in Nuits-St. Georges in Burgundy, not far from Dijon. That was not the shortest way, but Saskia had thought the strange name was worth a detour.

Their final destination was a little house near Hyères in the hills above the Mediterranean. They'd covered such distances in one day, but this time they had mainly stuck to the local roads, and instead of bypassing Paris on the freeway, they had driven straight through, and when they got lost they stopped for a drink at an outdoor café. "It's much more fun to watch the local color change slowly," Saskia had said.

The local color seems to turn red every time we get

to a traffic light, thought Rex, but, to his own surprise, he did not say it.

But it had been a long and hot drive, and during the past hour their mood had grown prickly. Saskia had to put her knitting aside twice in ten minutes because Rex asked to have an orange peeled and she dropped the second one on the floor.

"Ooh! It fell! Ooh!" she said.

She's doing that on purpose, Rex thought, but he said nothing. Maybe he had exaggerated his privileges as the driver, to rub it in that she never did her share. He had paid for her driving lessons, but once she passed the test, she almost never drove, no matter how much he urged her to. It was a disappointment; he had dreamed of endless trips together, spelling each other through the long nights.

Saskia put her head close to the dashboard.

"What are you doing?"

"Just checking the gas."

"We just filled the tank!"

"I was just checking."

The gas gauge of Rex's car was broken. It had already been broken three years ago during their first vacation together. One evening, he had ignored the last service station they passed, swearing that they had enough gas to reach the hotel—and Saskia had had to wait three hours on a pitch-black Italian country road until he returned with a jerry can. Since then a magnetized notepad had been stuck onto the dashboard to keep track of the mileage, a present from Saskia. On holiday trips she took care of that herself; there were already three numbers in her handwriting. They clearly showed that Nuits-St. Georges could be reached without refilling. Still, you were always a bit nervous on the first day of a vacation. So much could go wrong: Had the hotel reservation been received, were the bicycles secure on the roof of the car, did the little house they had rented really exist?

Why don't you get behind the wheel yourself? thought Rex, then you can see the odometer much better. And as he thought it, he said to himself, "I shouldn't say that," but he said it anyway.

"I'd rather not be stuck without gas again, if you don't mind," she snapped.

"We happen to have enough to drive all the way back to Amsterdam," said Rex.

Saskia whistled a few notes and looked out the window.

On a rise ahead of them, a gas station loomed up like a strange white castle, announced by a billboard: TOTAL 900 METERS. Next station: FINA 49 KILOMETERS. FINA would have been okay, but this TOTAL station stood there as an inevitable invitation to a quarrel.

They kept silent.

At the very last moment Rex swung into the driveway and up to the pumps. He hadn't even slowed down, just to take her by surprise.

God, how silly, he thought. He tried to catch Saskia's reaction out of the corner of his eye. She pinched her lips and widened her eyes, a comical grimace that had a special meaning for them: *Let's make up*.

They looked at each other and laughed.

"Peace?" she said, raising two fingers in the V sign.

"Peace."

"Okay, then, I'll take advantage of the situation to take a pee."

He had already decided to continue without filling up—every gas pump was occupied—but now Rex took his place at the end of the shortest line. Saskia gave him a kiss and got out.

I sure love that girl, he thought, as Saskia, with her basket over her arm, vanished through the automatic glass doors of the station. A smile appeared on his face and he quickly looked at it in the rearview mirror, as if it were a present from her. After four years it was still hard to believe that she was truly his.

Their childish bickering really showed how close they were; they indulged in it to feel how much they loved each other, like rich people throwing their money around. An hour from now they'd be sharing a bathtub in Nuits-St. Georges.

Even now, at ten past seven in the evening, it was still crowded by the gas pumps, with ice cream wrappers littering the ground, mobile homes, men in shorts and rumpled T-shirts, and a VW bug with a canoe called *Queen Elizabeth* on its roof. When it was finally Rex's turn to drive up to the pump he almost crushed a little Vietnamese-looking girl pulling a duck on wheels.

The automatic doors of the service station got little rest from a motley throng that had only one thing in common: The TOTAL station was no one's final destination. A black man in an African robe stood looking for someone while clutching two ice cream cones by their tips; a man with his arm in a sling was leaning against the glass wall of the store, scratching his head with his free hand; a father took a snapshot of a girl and boy who were wearing RICARD caps. And there, just as he was paying his bill, Saskia's crinkly hair appeared behind the window.

They both got in. Saskia looked at the mileage and wrote it down on the pad. She took more time than necessary, and when she had finished, Rex read: *512 (!!!) A little early, but who cares!* He kissed her above the ear and pulled away from the pump: now in one stretch to Nuits-St. Georges.

But Saskia said, "Shouldn't we rest here for a while? It would do you good. Come on, we were going to take it slow and easy."

Rex would really have preferred to go on now, but this wasn't the time to ignore her good intentions. He parked near a trash bin at the far end of the field that extended beyond the gas station.

Saskia emptied the orange peels from her bag into

the bin, and then they kicked and tossed a ball around that she had bought for him to relieve the stiffness from driving. After that, they walked with their arms around each other to the fence at the far end of the field and sat down on a little hill. Behind it was a large heap of garbage.

"Not really a refreshing pause near a babbling brook," Saskia said. There was a Milky Way of wrappings and empty cigarette packs stretching all the way to the pumps.

They sat together in silence for a while. Daylight was already waning, and through a hedge they could see the cars streaming along the turnpike—one could imagine them gliding by forever.

"Hey, I love you," said Saskia. The large red letters TOTAL over the roof of the gas station formed a plastic crown above her head.

"And I love you."

"And we're going to have a great vacation."

"Yes. Yes, I think so too."

"Shall we bury a coin here?"

"Yes."

Rex opened his wallet and handed Saskia a franc. She had one herself and shook the two coins in her cupped hands so you couldn't tell which was whose. She then chose one of the posts of the fence and buried the coins next to each other in a crack of the cement. Their edges remained visible and Rex covered them with a big pebble.

He counted the posts; it was the eighth from the end. It made him smile, for eight was her lucky number. Roses were most beautiful in bunches of eight, and she had always been sorry that he wasn't a year younger— then they would have been eight years apart.

He embraced her, and they held each other for a while.

"I'll drive next," Saskia said. "Okay?"

"Sure," said Rex.

He wasn't going to say anything sarcastic now, and sincerely hoped that nothing about him *looked* sarcastic.

"But first, I would like a cold drink. Wouldn't you? I'll get it. Shall I bring you something?"

"Let me go, then."

"No, I'd like to. My treat. Shall I get you a beer? After all, you won't be doing any more driving."

"That'd be great."

"Why don't you give me the keys, then I'll get used to the idea."

Rex handed her the keys with the frayed bit of leather, which once held a charm, and Saskia walked back over the Milky Way to the service station. He followed her with his eyes, in her jeans and yellow sweater stitched with gold thread. She often wore sweaters with low-cut backs, perhaps because he had once told her that her back was the most beautiful part of her body: obstinate, vulnerable, and freckled.

"You have money?" he called.

She turned back and held up her purse.

"Okay, then." He waved, and Saskia walked on.

The next time he looked she was gone.

He jumped up and down a few times, jogged around the field, and sat down once more. Peace-pee, getting used to the keys. . . . You phony, he thought. This was the fourth or fifth time they had buried coins together, and at least three times he'd looked her straight in the eye and thought, Crap. But it wasn't that he just *tolerated* these things; they were also the things that made him love her. How was that possible?

One morning when she was still asleep, he had opened her bag and taken out a guilder. Trembling, yet at the same time fascinated by his own evil, he had just stood there with the money in his hand and didn't put it back. Another time he had needed a quote from a book that he couldn't find right away but knew she also owned. As he dialed her number he suddenly remembered where his own copy was, but later he had called her anyway. And as she dictated the passage to him, and he read along in his own copy, he experienced a frightening pleasure. He had never told her about this; it was the biggest secret he kept from her.

These were tortures—why? He had never done such things to any other girlfriend. Saskia was the only one with whom he had really wanted to be *one*—had he tormented her because he realized that even with her this would never be possible?

An interesting theory, but he'd better watch his step or he might lose her with all his pestering.

Rex got up and went back to the car. He took the Polaroid camera out of Saskia's basket and took a picture of the service station. A joke for when she'd return, but he could imagine the effect on friends, on Saskia, and on himself years from now when they would read the caption in the picture album: *TOTAL gas station with Saskia inside, a few minutes before she will drive on the Autoroute for the first time.*

Holding the Polaroid by one corner, he saw the TOTAL station and the parked cars emerge from the chemicals as if for a moment they were alive. He put the camera back in the car and with the photo in his hand sauntered back to their hill where no mountain stream was babbling. He sat down, leaned back on his elbows, and looked at the service station.

Perhaps teasing her about running out of gas had gone too far. That night on the country road in Italy was not just about having to wait for three hours. When he finally got back with his jerry can, he had found Saskia in a terrible state. She had clung to him like a cornered animal, sobbing that he should never leave her alone like that again. The confinement inside the small black compartment of the car had almost driven her out of her mind with fear; it had been as lonely as her nightmare about the golden egg.

Once, as a little girl, she had dreamed that she was locked inside a golden egg that flew through the universe. Everything was pitch-black, there weren't even any stars, she'd have to stay there forever, and she couldn't even die. There was only one hope. Another golden egg was flying through space. If it collided with her own, both would be destroyed, and everything would be over. But the universe was so vast!

It had been shocking to Rex that a little girl could have had such a terrifying vision. And yet that was what he had teased her about!

He looked at his watch: just after seven-thirty. Above the treetops across the turnpike hung the soft violet wisps of mist that always made her say, "Look, tomorrow will be a beautiful day." Such predictions were far from sure, of course, and their little house was still a whole day's drive away, but Rex saluted the wisps in her spirit: This would be an unforgettable holiday, brimming with sunlight. They also predict, he thought, that I will avoid all opportunities to tease her for the rest of the vacation.

What a darling she was, really, offering to drive, but by dragging her feet she was making it very clear how reluctant she was. Rex got up once more, did some kicking exercises, and skipped back to the car.

Her flowered jacket hung over the back of her seat, the visor was lowered on her side. It almost always was, a running little joke between them, for it had a mirror.

"If you're gonna drive, you gotta look beautiful"; he could hear her say it. She was probably doing an elaborate makeup job in the ladies' room. She made no bones about being vain, Rex had even managed to take a picture of her standing on a snowy beach in a driving wind, against a background of dark clouds: Her pants clung to her legs and streaks of snowflakes chased about as she took out a pocket mirror and put on lipstick. But this vanity of hers took away none of the wanton, tragic beauty of her face.

She had taken money with her, hadn't she? Yes, for if she hadn't she would have returned sooner. And she had shown him her purse.

He took a few more turns on the lawn, waving his arms, filling his lungs. He looked at his watch. The wisps of mist had turned from violet to purple and were growing still darker.

I'm sure getting a chance to put my good intentions into practice, thought Rex. So I will *not* go and sit behind the wheel looking grumpy; forget it, just hand me the keys. I will *not* put the beer away she's bringing me so sweetly. I will *not* drive back to the pumps and wait for her there. Besides, she has the keys.

He looked at his watch. Nineteen minutes to eight. He leaned against the car for a while, stared at the TOTAL building, and then took the Polaroid out of his breast pocket. It was no longer the same scene. One or two cars had gone, a new one had driven up, all the people had changed places.

Now she was really overdoing it. Should he go wake her up out of the fashion magazine she was probably leafing through? No, it was just like her to be picking

flowers behind the gas station if she had seen some
growing there, or she might be choosing a present for
him. It would be something like a baby pacifier, or one
of those whistles on a string that make bird noises when
you whirl them around, or the tiniest possible notebook
with a useless little pencil, and he would think, Get lost
with that stuff, and yet he'd be delighted with his present, and admire it in all sincerity and feel happy that
she belonged to him.

How long had she actually been gone?

Seventeen minutes to eight. Rex could not suppress
a sense of alarm. What a nuisance that he couldn't lock
the car, or he'd definitely go and have a look.

He would wait until the second hand had made one
more lap around the dial. Then, without giving it any
more thought, he threw his wallet into her basket and,
taking it under his arm, ran to the fuel pumps.

"The car is dying to be driven by you." That was
what he would say; not something grumpy about having
to abandon it.

The glass doors jumped open for him as he entered
the service station. Across from the entrance was the
cash register and to the right was the food area. She
wasn't there. He had saved looking to the left for last:
Now he had to do it. On either side of a central counter
holding Eiffel towers and puzzles were two aisles that
led to the soda machines and a pinball machine. She was
not there. To the right of the machine was a corridor
leading to the toilets. She wasn't there either. He

opened the door to the ladies' room; she was not standing in front of the mirror.

Rex hurried back outside and walked behind the rear of the service station, where there was another, smaller parking lot, and a narrow extension of the field with two wooden picnic tables and benches. No flowers grew in the grass and she was not there.

He raced back to the car. He stood there, out of breath, at a total loss.

A hollow emptiness spread through his belly, as if he were sitting on a swing that did not stop going down. Something had gone wrong, he could tell by the cheerful colors of the bicycles on the roof, the colors in her jacket. Suddenly he felt totally alone, as if it was all over.

Was she teasing him? Impossible.

He took a pad and pen out of the bag that held the reading material for the holidays and, using the hood of the car, which was still warm, he wrote: *Sas, I've lost you. I'm looking for you. If you come here, stay near the car. Rex XXX.* He stuck the slip of paper under the windshield wiper.

Once more he looked at the photograph. Only a large white trailer truck remained; "Amaddei Frères," it said.

The basket still on his arm, he walked slowly back to the station. Through the hedge shone the yellow glow of the first cars on the turnpike that had switched on their headlights.

Once more. Systematically he sifted the building for

her possible presence. She was not to the right, not in the two aisles, nor near the soda machines. He entered the ladies' room. A Hindu woman stood washing her hands and stared at him suspiciously. Of the three toilets one was occupied. He pulled open the doors of the two empty ones and waited for the third. A small woman came out who looked like a caricature of his last girlfriend. She said something loud and shrill, of which he grasped only that it was French.

He searched the men's room.

Across from the entrance to the ladies' room was a door marked "SERVICE," and underneath, in smaller lettering, a notice not to enter. Rex opened the door. A man sitting behind a desk looked up, annoyed.

"This is not accessible to the public," he said.

Rex excused himself and closed the door.

Now what?

She was not in the station. Then she must have returned to the car; his note would keep her there. He walked back to the car, which was now a shadowy silhouette, with the bikes on the roof like awkward antlers. The note stuck under the windshield wiper moved softly in a breeze that was otherwise unnoticeable. She had not added a message to his.

She seemed to have vanished from the face of the earth.

Rex sat down on the sidewalk near the trash bin. A prince in a white Rolls-Royce? One mad impulse and vroom, right past him, into a brand-new life? "I'm a bit of a weather vane," she had told him often enough—she might have realized in a flash that he was not, and never would be, perfect for her. But to leave him like this? Unthinkable.

Now the very last moment that something normal could still have happened was passsing.

He stood up and began to call, "Saskia, Saskia!" Nothing happened, except for his voice dying away against the eternal roar of the turnpike.

Two minutes to eight. By now the field had turned brownish, and the wisps of mist had disappeared. Continuously calling her name, Rex returned to the gas station, where the huge Amaddei Frères trailer truck was taking off, wheezing and shaking. Had she been dragged inside it and raped? Was she being carried off to be dumped somewhere along the road? He screamed, "Saskia, Saskia, Saskia!" and walked back to the rear of the service station. Behind the picnic tables and the fence was a ditch. He stepped into it and waded about, searching the bottom with his feet. He stopped. Things couldn't be so bad that he should be looking for Saskia in ditches.

She had to be *somewhere*. Only: He was not allowed to know where. It was intolerable, humiliating.

He went to the pumps and stood on the sidewalk in front of the automatic doors. Keeping his eyes riveted on the evasive face of a young pump attendant, he called, "Saskia! Saskia!" People froze on the spot.

"It's my wife. She's disappeared," he said, half expecting the attendant to interrupt his work and see to it that Saskia would return.

Rex entered the store just as the neon lights flickered on. It was no longer crowded. Even if Saskia had been here, there was no one left who would have seen her.

Except for the cashier! And suddenly he remembered that in a dark little corner of his wallet he had a picture of her.

It was a picture in which she pouted coquettishly, but the cashier recognized her at once. "Isn't her hair shorter now? Sure, I saw her a while ago." She said that Saskia had been standing near the coffee machine, and a bit later she had come to get change. About half an hour ago.

So she *had* come inside to buy drinks; her first steps after he'd lost sight of her! But the coffee machine? She had gone to get him a beer, and a soda for herself. And yet the cashier was quite certain it had been coffee, she was sure of it, and it was unlikely that she had made a mistake. The coffee and soft-drink machines stood far apart in opposite corners, with ice cream and pinball machines in between. Had there been someone with her? Had she talked to anyone? The cashier hadn't paid such close attention. It was possible. Hundreds of people walked in and out of there all day long. . . .

"She has disappeared," said Rex. "I don't know what to do."

The cashier looked worried. There wasn't anything else she could remember.

Rex stood in the open space in front of the cash register and held up his photograph. "Ladies and gentlemen, could you please help me?" he said to everyone. "My wife disappeared from here. Half an hour ago. She came in to buy something and never returned. Would you please look at this photograph and tell me if you saw her?"

He had spoken French, then repeated it in English. The few people in the shop stood in silence like polite onlookers at a memorial service in a foreign country. When Rex was finished they continued on their way.

A small balding man was the only one who actually looked at the snapshot. Rex recognized him. It was the man who had been sitting at the desk behind the door to the office, the manager of the TOTAL station.

Back in his office, Rex told him what had happened. The manager wrote down Saskia's vital statistics, then called the police. He repeated everything word for word, right down to the last letter of her address. He said *"Oui"* a few times, then hung up. The police would not come. A disappearance of forty-five minutes? Short-staffed as they were? "I take you seriously, sir. You know that you didn't have a fight with your wife. But how can the police be certain? Let's try again in an hour."

"What do you think could have happened?" asked Rex.

He was allowed to call the hotel in Nuits-St. Georges for free. Among the various objects in Saskia's basket—a sweater, a pocket mirror, an apple, a half-eaten roll of licorice—he found the tourist folder with all the addresses. The hotel was called Côte d'Or; the manager looked up the number for him.

The casual voice of the receptionist shocked him, if only by the fact that it existed at all. Saskia had not arrived, and Rex warned the receptionist that she might be coming alone.

Accompanied by the manager he made the rounds of the gas-pump attendants. And Saskia took her next step: Of the three attendants who thought they had seen her, one had watched her come out through the glass doors, holding a can in each hand.

And then?

For the life of me, the man seemed to say. Had there been anyone near her? No one in particular.

So she had been within calling distance! If he had been standing near the car he would have been able to see her! But he *had* been standing there, and he had even taken a photograph! Rex ran back inside.

Could he possibly have made the Polaroid just as she was coming out? Standing near a rack that held yellow Michelin road maps, he held the photograph up to the light.

The entrance to the store was dark. It was hard to make out, but it looked as if the top of the Amaddei truck hid the door. Farther on, a few passenger cars stood near the trash bins, their trunks or their hoods open, and a few were parked in the lot directly in front of the store. People were lying or sitting in the grass, others stood near their cars. Rex counted a total of seventeen people, or dots that might be people. He was certain that ten of them were not Saskia. Could she possibly be one of the other dots? Beside a green car were two pinpricks silhouetted against the white Amaddei Frères truck. Could one of these be called reddish?

The cashier called him back, for she remembered something else. For what it was worth. Saskia had been clumsy when getting her change because she was clutching a bunch of car keys at the same time. She had even dropped them once. There had been no one with her at the register.

Rex went outside and, passing the spot where the two pinpricks had been, walked slowly to his car, which had almost disappeared in the twilight. At first glance he could tell that something was wrong, but he didn't believe it until he stood right next to the car: The bikes had been stolen. Some of the straps with which they had been fastened lay on the luggage rack.

He sat down on the curb, next to a fluorescent-blue plastic garbage bag that rustled in the evening breeze.

"Where *are* you?" he said and began to cry uncontrollably. "I will see you again, won't I?" He felt as lonely as an abandoned spacewalker.

He got into the car and turned on the cabin light. Her things were still in their places: the jacket hanging on the back of her seat, her knitting on top of her book in the glove compartment, and next to it the pad: *512 (!!!) A little early, but who cares!*

A cigarette butt with lipstick on it stuck out of the ashtray; her cigarettes and lighter lay next to her book. Rex lit one and inhaled, his first smoke in seven years. A slight dizziness spread across his neck and forehead.

She had been gone for over an hour. He could visualize her, frightened, breathing through her nose. This could no longer be merely a misunderstanding about which they would have a good laugh. Whatever had happened to her, she was certain to be in danger. He went wild with grief that he could not help her.

If he thought about it clearly, there was only one realistic explanation. She must have been dragged or tricked into a car and kidnapped. She looked sexy, but not wealthy. Perhaps her abductor had even noticed that she belonged with Rex's shabby old car. So he must have had rape in mind. She was probably being raped at this very moment. And after that? She might well be murdered, and sooner or later her body would be found. But surely she would not have been so stupid as to resist. There was a good chance that she might be dropped off in some lonely spot, and after a while she would be able to reach the hotel. All in all, that was the likeliest scenario. Perhaps their holiday could even be salvaged.

With her basket on his arm, Rex reconstructed her

movements since he had last seen her. He clocked her. Into the store, to the soda machines, looking for francs, getting change—all done rather slowly—getting out two cans. Then to the coffee machine? Had she had a sudden longing for coffee?

Sure, why not? Okay, drink coffee, go outside, pose for a final snapshot.

The times all checked out: He might have taken her picture. But it was impossible to tell from the photograph itself.

The manager called the police. Rex had to take the phone, and for the first time in her life someone had to give the police a description of Saskia.

He waited. With the phone against his ear, he watched the manager copying numbers from a loose-leaf notebook into a register. After an endless delay, the voice returned: Saskia Ehlvest had not been brought to any of the hospitals in the area. Nothing could be done now; it was too dark to search and perhaps she would return on her own within the next few hours. If she still hadn't shown up by morning he should call them back, and they would investigate. He was told not to call before eight A.M.

Night had fallen.

The cashier left. The pump attendant who had been the last to see her went home to sleep. Rex was now the only one in the entire station who had ever seen Saskia. He called the hotel but she did not come and she did not come. He called the police: She was still not registered in any hospital.

Rex walked in circles around his car and the station but she was never there when he came back. Only rarely did the Autoroute yield up a car, and a softly buzzing silence descended over the TOTAL station.

Just as had been predicted by her wisps of mist, the night was clear and pure, endless. She had to be *somewhere*. It broke his heart not to know where.

Finally he just sat in the car staring at the pad with its numbers and at the note under the windshield wiper, one corner fluttering in the breeze. To want to sleep, to be unable to sleep, to sleep, it all merged into a single thought: Something dreadful was happening to Saskia at this very moment. It was as if he could feel what she was now feeling—the terror and the loneliness of the Golden Egg—and as if, in doing so, his wish had finally been fulfilled to be one with her.

2

The water of the inlet was as blue as if painted by a child. Rex Hofman stood on a rock at the side and looked at the horizon through the keyhole of rocky walls. He wondered how the earth and moon managed to create four-feet-high waves elsewhere in this sea, while here it remained without a ripple.

The inlet was no more than a cove created by the rocks, and the sun reached it only a few hours each day, early in the morning. The little beach had sand of a rare fineness, so silvery that the grains looked like tiny diamonds. It was narrow in both directions, and at the foot of the rocks of the back wall grew thistles and wild cactuses with fiery red flowers.

Clashing with those natural colors was their bright orange rubber boat with outboard motor that brought them there every morning. The beach could not be reached on foot and was hard to find even by boat. To preserve this exclusivity they made sure that no one followed them when they left the fishing harbor. Successfully, they were always alone.

Rex shouted and waved toward the little beach and dove in. The water surrounded him with silence, except for a hissing sound as of millions of glass needles touching his head and shattering. His arms in front of him, hands folded, he let himself float. His eyes were closed, and he felt neither his body nor the water; it was as if he could drift on like this forever.

Then he lifted his head back into the world and swam slowly to the beach.

Lieneke lay reading on her stomach, halfway under the umbrella. Rex kneeled next to her and took a cigarette. She shivered from the drops of water that fell on her back, where they became small, glistening magnifying glasses. She put her book facedown in the sand and turned toward him.

"Have a good swim?"

"Delicious. Divine. I'll fall asleep underwater here."

She smiled as if he'd paid her a compliment. Marina di Camerota belonged to her, or rather, to her family. She'd played on this idyllic little beach when she was two and until not so long ago she'd been back countless times with her parents. They owned a small house on the hill above the harbor, with a splendid view of the Gulf of Policastro. Now she and Rex had borrowed it along with the rubber boat and its trailer.

He took a bottle of beer out of the cooler and handed her one too.

"Those drops on your back, do they really give you freckles when you lie in the sun?" he asked.

"Oh, I think that's just an old wives' tale," said Lieneke.

"You think so? Yes, I think so too."

Lieneke was busy reading still another book. She had started it that morning and while he hadn't done more than glance at the paper and take a dive, she had already reached page 125. She continued reading; Rex sat on a rock, letting his legs dangle in the water. Since the inlet didn't have any tides, it was always the same depth. Camerota was indeed a find. Hardly any tourists, only one windsurfer. No one ever cheated or shortchanged you here: just one hour's drive south of Naples, all the clichés about Italy were proved wrong. One day Rex was about to drive out of the harbor parking lot with his wallet still lying on the roof of the car and a couple of teenage boys had stopped him and handed it back to him.

Perhaps he enjoyed a special consideration here because he was with Lieneke. She spoke perfect Italian and knew everyone, and everyone knew her. And whenever she introduced him to still another old pizza baker, and they laughed together at his incomprehensible sentences, Rex felt as safe as a little boy holding his mother's hand.

With a fresh cigarette in his mouth and his toes performing dance steps in the water, Rex daydreamed about the three "dragons" he had vowed to slay in Camerota: Lieneke, Vicenze, and the French.

Lieneke was already in the bag. At the beginning of

the holiday he had taught her a word game that he had played all his life: with his parents, with schoolmates during geography class, with girlfriends. Lieneke had paid close attention to his explanation and then proceeded to win the first game. It had irritated Rex more than he let on. While she raced through her summer reading, he had been groggy from the sun and abandoned his first book at page forty; that was enough of an admission of her greater lucidity—or his own decline. It was *his* game; he had a quarter of a century's practice. But he had won the next game and all the succeeding ones; it had been beginner's luck. His victories shone even brighter in the light of her annoyance.

The second dragon was Vicenze, and he too had been slain by Rex. Above the harbor, within the old fortress wall, was a barren and ill-attended café, an enormous granite room where chairs screeched icily when you moved them. It was the only café in Camerota with a video game, and in the evening, before or after dinner, and sometimes both, Rex tried to beat his own record while Lieneke patiently drank beer and read.

Every now and then he had an opponent, a little boy named Vicenze, whose name sometimes appeared on the screen when his score earned him the right to type it in. Vicenze always brought along his own footstool so that he could reach the buttons, and then stood there completely absorbed, firing at space monsters that attacked his spaceship with rumbling and hissing sounds.

They couldn't play together very often because Vicenze absolutely refused to have his turn paid for. He was only eight, he once said, to explain his lack of money and perhaps his many defeats. Rex asked him when his birthday was, and from the resulting conversation, during which Vicenze was very patient, he learned that the right word was *compleanno*, not *anniversario*.

"You're good, kid," he muttered, but one thing was certain: In Marina di Camerota the Dutchman Rex Hofman was the best destroyer of space monsters.

The third dragon was the French. He hadn't entered the ring with them yet. He longed to do so but wondered whether the occasion would ever arise.

"Ready for another word game?" Lieneke asked.

Together they pushed the rubber boat into the water. Lieneke started the motor and took the rudder, and Rex stretched out opposite her. With arms and knees spread wide, he lay against the bow, looking at the sky through his eyelashes and staring at her small face that always looked slightly surprised.

That is Lieneke, he thought, what to make of her, really? Finally pick a quarrel to see if there is a tie worth breaking? Wait for her to leave of her own accord? Study her devotion like a biologist trying to understand the language of seagulls?

The boat began to rock heavily. They had left the cove and were now at sea. Lieneke had put on her black bikini and buttoned a blue shirt over it, for paradise was still a bit prudish.

The French were already there, as they were every afternoon when Rex and Lieneke arrived at the main beach. Here the sand was less fine, there were flattened soda cans scattered about, and, from the campground, no farther than a cactus-bordered path away, you could hear Italian pop songs. But it wasn't really any less idyllic.

They greeted the French and threw their towels on the sand a little farther down. These French, three in all, belonged to the same two minorities as Rex and Lieneke; they had no children with them and they were foreigners. They were hard to place: two men in their thirties and a Chinese or Vietnamese girl. One could imagine them as drug dealers, but also as young left-wing lawyers, or maybe members of a rock group.

One of the men was tall and thin, but compared with the two others he was rather nondescript. The Asian girl was small, with a body like a child's. She was the only woman on the beach who sometimes left off her bikini top, but her nudity was so natural that it would have been obscene to take offense. She might just as well be sixteen as thirty, and it was unclear with which man she belonged.

The other man was fat and completely bald. He wore glasses, and with his thick, white lips he looked like a

Mongolian. "That bald head is a trick," Lieneke said, "to make you believe that that's what makes him so ugly."

The bald man wore large swimming trunks of an almost indecent yellow, and when the other two went swimming, he followed them wearily but with a certain elegance. He then sat down in the shallows and let the waves slap about him, like a flabby Burmese prince on a throne.

He couldn't swim!

They had been greeting one another with a half-raised hand and a mumbled word for two weeks now, and Rex was beginning to feel sorry that they hadn't gotten closer. By now it was obvious that they were not the kind of people who immediately exchanged addresses and got together for barbecues; and some fresh conversation wouldn't do any harm.

The confrontation, if it ever came to that, would take place high up on the beach. A kind of playing field had been made there, the beach cleared of thistles, with a rope stretched between two stakes, which was supposed to be the net. Stones marked the four corners. Rex had an old badminton set that they faithfully brought to the beach every time, but because of the word games, the reading, and general laziness, they had batted the shuttlecock around only once, and not for more than fifteen minutes.

The Frenchmen, on the other hand, could be found on the court every day. They too had a badminton set, and by late afternoon, when the shadow of the high rocks pushed the swimmers back to the campground, they would take up their rackets.

Resting his chin on his fists, Rex would watch them from a distance.

They weren't very good at it, but they played seriously, keeping score and whenever they weren't sure whether the shuttle had passed over or under the rope, they looked at the girl, a silent umpire, and accepted her verdict. The bald man played slowly but tenaciously, and as far as Rex could tell, he and the tall one were about equal in strength.

I should be able to beat those guys, thought Rex. Should he just ask them if he could join?

The notepads were ready for the next word game, two beers had been opened, the Frenchmen went to the field. But this time they threw down their rackets and, bending down and crawling on the ground, they started clearing the field of stones, tossing them outside the imaginary borders of the court. Suddenly Rex saw a ploy to engage this third dragon.

"Just a minute," he said, and ran toward the field.

"Can I help?" he asked. "We play here too sometimes." He had addressed himself to the bald man, who looked surprisingly boyish from close up, with merry little eyes. Perhaps he was only in his twenties after all.

"Bohh," he said with a shrug.

The four of them silently threw stones into the thistles.

"I wanted to ask you," said Rex, "what about a match,
France against Holland? My girlfriend plays too. European championship," he added with a grin.

The girl kept score, the men were France. It didn't seem
to make any difference that they had had a lot more
practice, everyone played equally poorly and most of
the rallies were quickly decided by a ridiculous miss.
But, as if it were meant to be, Rex and Lieneke took a
6–0 early lead. After that, luck ran more evenly, and
they ended up winning the first set 15 to 10.

They changed sides, and in the second set Rex and
Lieneke again took the lead, now always by one or two
points. Lieneke turned out to have a good feel for the
game, and to Rex's delight she took the match seriously.
When the Vietnamese girl ruled a shot of hers *in* that
she had feared *out,* she showed her relief by clenching
her fist, and when she and Rex scored a crucial point,
she made a face that he recognized from many years
ago, before she was born. It was the way his teammates
on the junior soccer team had looked at one another
when they were in the lead: "Okay now, boys, don't let
it slip!"

This is Lieneke, this is how she is, thought Rex.

It felt like a violation of something predestined, but
the French made a comeback. The score was 12–12, 13–13,
and, because Rex made a number of mistakes by calling

out "Let go" on shots that he should have left to Lieneke, the second set suddenly ended with a 15–13 victory
for France. A third set would be decisive.

This time it was close from the beginning. No one
laughed or talked. The girl counted the score in a
monotonous voice. When it was 8–7 for France, they
changed sides. Although the misses became more and
more numerous and ridiculous, the teams kept pace
with each other.

Okay, thought Rex. The outcome of this match
means something. If we win, I'll marry her.

The boldness of this plan overwhelmed him and he
missed a shot because he was daydreaming about how
he would tell his children, when they were old enough,
that a simple game of badminton had decided their
existence.

"Don't let it slip away now," Lieneke nodded to him,
shaking her fist.

"Maybe I will marry her, you know," Rex said to
Saskia, who was observing them, kneeling on the side-
lines, her straw basket by her side in the sand.

But it seemed as if a diabolical force had taken hold
of the match, keeping the score even. It was 15–15, 16–16;
as if they had become a binary star the two teams soared
to ever higher scores. The bald man had a chance to
finish the match with one easy stroke, but hit with the
frame; a winning hit of Rex's landed just behind a corner stone; at match point he just missed the shut-

tlecock—thanks to a desperate backhand of Lieneke's, they survived.

I'll do it, thought Rex.

18–18, 19–19, 22–22, it was totally ridiculous, but it seemed as if nothing could be done about it.

France vs. Holland had been going on for at least forty-five minutes; the shadow of the rock had reached the playing field and started creeping up their ankles. Exhausted, the players tottered about in the soft sand, their bodies gleaming with sweat. No one could hit the shuttle properly anymore. When he missed a return, the bald man fell under the rope at Rex's feet, within smelling distance, his peeling scalp covered with little drops of sweat.

"Pouhff," he said.

25–25: Had anything like this ever happened before? It was frightening, as if chance were mocking them, as if doing their best was beside the point—and although he knew his fate was at stake, Rex could barely suppress a hysterical giggle.

So reliable had this balancing force seemed that no one could believe it when the bald man missed a perfectly easy lob by Lieneke and the game suddenly came to an end: 15–10, 13–15, and 30–28 for Holland. Astonished, they all stared at the shuttlecock that had remained upright on a pile of sand, like a moon lander on display.

"Yes!" exclaimed Lieneke.

Fifteen minutes later they were all drinking wine outside the Frenchmen's tent. They were musicians, members of a punk-rock group from Lille called Far Out. The tall one was the guitarist and lead singer, the girl his girlfriend, and the bald one the drummer.

As Rex leaned back and studied the wisps of mist above the pier, Lieneke was discussing their victory meal with the proprietress. None of the restaurants in Marina di Camerota had a real menu, cooks and clients alike were dependent on the day's catch. It didn't make any difference: Delicious dishes always arrived at the table, fish with untranslatable names that swam only in the Gulf of Policastro.

The conversation that evening did not go as smoothly as usual, nor did the silences. Rex had to admit he was as shy as a schoolboy about broaching the subject that fate had determined That darling Lieneke sat there, spearing yet another fish with her fork, unaware of what he had in mind. That was cruel; he had to remedy this quickly. Below the terrace of the restaurant, a late fishing boat came in—whatever made him so certain that she would have *him*?

"I really enjoyed the badminton," said Lieneke. "And I loved it that we won!" She was silent for a long time. Then, looking up at Rex with a hesitant, slightly sorrowful expression, she said, "I don't exactly know how to put this, but at a certain point I got the feeling that the outcome would have a special significance." She looked down at her fish.

"Hold it," said Rex. "I'm ashamed. That is exactly what I was going to say. Why are men always so much more cowardly about such things than women?" He looked her straight in the eyes. A tuft of rebellious hair that no hairdresser had ever been able to tame stood straight up on top of her head; it had accompanied her from one photo album to another.

"I feel crazy enough to marry you," he said. "I don't know if you are crazy enough too . . . ?" Did that really sound logical?

Lieneke looked out over the little harbor. "I was conceived in this place, did you know?"

"Really?"

"I'd marry you too, I guess."

"You would?"

"Yes."

They both laughed, then fell silent. They continued eating. There were no fish knives in Marina di Camerota. In the kitchen the big hit of that summer was playing on the radio, appropriate to the occasion as all Italian pop songs and proving that no one should feel superior to even the most obvious sentimentality.

"Real conversation killers, these marriage proposals," said Lieneke.

"Yes."

She held out her hand, and he took it in his own. They looked at each other and grinned.

"Do you know what I was thinking in the café while you were playing? Who to have as witnesses. All right, shall we get married? Sometime in February?"

"Okay," said Rex. "I've got an erection. Do you know what kind of erection? Not a sexual one, it has nothing to do with that. It's like the feeling I had when I smoked my first cigarette with a friend. An erection from the thrill, from doing something exciting. That's what this feels like with you. It is exciting because it is something new, but also because I am violating laws that are still in effect. And you know what they're about. And you also know that we have to discuss that now."

"Saskia."

"Yes."

"Do you think about her often?" She swallowed.

"At least once a day."

Lieneke was silent. Her fork slipped, making a shrill sound on the plate.

"Did you ever mention marriage to her?"

"Oh, yes. But we were just kidding. She was much too young."

"She was a year older than I am now!"

"You're different. And I'm different. Of course we would have gotten married. And divorced, long ago. Or maybe not. That's not what it's about."

"I know. You see, I've never dared mention Saskia."

The table was being cleared, they drank wine and smoked, and with each new cigarette Lieneke added to her average of one a day. The proprietress skipped her usual chat. "I've never dared ask you, because I could only think of stupid questions. I can't imagine what it must be like for you."

"I don't mind your asking stupid questions."

She paused for a moment, as if taking a running jump into this territory.

"Do you have a picture of her with you?"

"That's not a stupid question. Yes. Do I ever look at it? No."

"Where do you keep it?"

"In my wallet, folded away somewhere."

"What kind of person was she?"

"Herself. A little difficult. Beautiful and sexy, and she liked to vacuum because of the funny way the cord whipped back in. The usual banalities, really. You feel love mostly in the pain. She never gave me a chance not to love her. Sometimes I think that's pretty presumptuous of her."

"Do you know what I did once? I went to a news agency and read their file on her."

"Really?" He covered her hand with his. "Sweetheart, I would have shown you mine."

"I didn't dare ask."

"It wouldn't have made any difference. Mine is probably bigger, but it wouldn't tell you any more."

"You said I could ask stupid questions. Do you ever hope she'll come back?"

"No. But I imagine it sometimes, and it always leaves me somewhat disappointed. As if I had lived these eight years in vain. I'm going to say something really cheap: If she came back I'd stay with you. But if I could go back to that service station I would. I say that honestly, because it makes no sense to have this conversation and not be honest."

"I don't mind." She smiled at him bravely.

"But do you know what the worst thing is? It's not knowing. Standing by that door with two sodas, and zip, gone! As if someone had decided that her atoms didn't belong together anymore. To have lost her makes sense, but not this not knowing. That is unbearable. You can play all kinds of mind games. For instance, I am told that she is alive somewhere and perfectly happy. And I'm given a choice: She goes on living like that, or I get to know everything and she dies. Then I let her die."

His story was getting too heavy; he let it race on in his head. He hoped he'd get the chance to change the subject; and he was grateful that Lieneke didn't ask the further questions she had.

Finally it was the French who helped them out. They were walking by along the waterfront, which was now in darkness, and they were so quiet that they had almost passed before Rex and Lieneke noticed them.

They raised their glasses.

The tall man and his girlfriend greeted them with a wave of the hand and a slight nod. The bald one followed them dreamily without looking up.

"Too bad we didn't take a picture of all of us together," said Rex.

"I know a good way to fix that," said Lieneke. "They come from Lille, right? It's not that far. Let's ask them to play at our wedding."

"Far out!" said Rex.

They laughed. Now the proprietress did intrude on their conversation. She insisted that Lieneke tell her what all the mysterious talk was about, and when she found out, she kissed her and Rex and, without asking, put three glasses of cheap champagne on the table.

Lieneke heard a sound that did not belong in the chirping, rustling nights of Marina di Camerota. It was very near, a tortured, frightening sound that woke her with a start.

It was Rex. He had talked in his sleep before, but this was completely different, a kind of moaning that scared her out of her wits. It sounded like "Gahd, gahd," plaintive cries that grew louder and then turned into sobs.

She tried to shake him awake but he shoved her away and cried, "No! No! Gaahd!" His screams reverberated in the tiled room, pleading, as if he were in terrible pain.

Chills ran up and down her back; she had touched heavy, ice-cold sweat. She saw his face in the pale light that came through the windows—his eyes were open wide.

"Darling, darling, what is it?"

"Gahd, gahd! The golden egg!"

"Rex, love, wake up for God's sake. What's this about a golden egg? You're having a nightmare. Shall I get you a cold towel?"

"Horrible! Horrible!" His voice seemed to come from so deep inside that she turned away from him with disgust. What could she do? She could only wait for his nightmare to end. But for how long would she be able to stand these inhuman sobs?

She realized she herself was crying; her pillow was soaked with tears.

3

In 1950 Raymond Lemorne was sixteen years old.

One weekend when he and his mother went to stay with his aunt and uncle in Dijon, the grown-ups went away on Sunday morning, leaving him alone in the apartment. It was on the second floor of the building and he put a kitchen chair out on the back balcony and began to read a book. After a while he put it down and leaned out over the railing. It overlooked a mowed lawn intersected by two paths leading to the next building. What if I jumped, he thought.

Music was playing somewhere else in the building, jazz violin, perhaps Stéphane Grappelli? He knew little about music. Chemistry was his favorite subject; he wanted to become a teacher.

He climbed on the chair and sat on the railing. Dangling his legs over the edge, his hands resting on his thighs, he looked at the grass below. The neighbor played one record after another, all jazz, nice to hear. It was June, the sun was shining, the sky was a stern blue.

Did the atmosphere turn with the earth or was it an immobile hollow sphere within which the earth rotated?

Raymond Lemorne felt completely happy. He was looking forward to the last two weeks of the school year. He was wearing short pants and a plaid shirt, open at the collar, and the wind felt cool against his skin. Every now and then the height made him shiver. Of course the atmosphere turned with the earth! What a fool he was—how could there be sea and land climates otherwise? And what storms there would be! At least one hundred on the Beaufort scale; he ought to figure that out one day. The earth would be swept flat, like a billiard ball in a polishing machine!

He thought about what would happen if he jumped. He considered the pros and cons, with a dark feeling at the back of his mind that it had already been decided that he would jump. But how could this be true if jumping was such obvious madness? And yet the idea had come up; how could that be if jumping wasn't at least a *possibility*? And how could he find out whether it was true that he had that possibility—except by actually jumping?

A Gordian knot of the mind!

He sat on the railing for an hour and a half, thinking about this contradiction, and about other things, and then jumped. He spent six weeks in the hospital with a broken leg and a compound fracture of his arm.

• • •

Twenty-one years went by before a similar idea occurred to Lemorne.

By then he was a chemistry teacher, married, and the father of two daughters aged thirteen and eleven. He was living in Autun, in the district of Saône-et-Loire, and taught at the local high school. One beautiful autumn Sunday he took his family on an outing to the Canal de Bourgogne, somewhere between Dijon and Beaune. They walked on a towpath along the edge of the wide, straight waterway, where no cars could come. In the low sun, the water was a dark green, like rotten spinach. Every now and then a barge slid by, majestic in its stillness. They were long, flat boats with only the steering cabin rising up above the deck, and almost always a small passenger car parked on the tar-black loading hatches.

One barge lay moored against the bank. As they walked past it, Lemorne heard a dull, splattering sound, as if a wounded duck were trying in vain to take off.

"There's a child in the water!" his daughters called out.

Lemorne ran down the bank and jumped into the water. By the stern of the ship a small face was bobbing up and down. It drifted to the middle of the canal, and danced in the wave of an approaching ship. With a few strokes, Lemorne reached those waves and grabbed the child. He swam back to shore, where his wife and daughters helped him onto dry land.

The child was a little girl wearing a checked dress.

She was conscious. Lemorne lay her down on the grass, and after a few moments she stood up.

"Where's Bidule?" she asked.

"Bidule? Who's that?"

"It's Bidule! He drowned!" A frown of despair appeared on her face, she was on the verge of tears. Lemorne understood that she was talking about a doll that had fallen into the water.

He took her hand and together they walked back to the ship.

A man and a woman came down the gangplank, gesticulating like scarecrows who suddenly discover they are alive. The woman was crying, and picked up the little girl. Lemorne's daughters began to cry as well.

A moment later they were all sitting in the cabin drinking coffee, Lemorne dressed in the skipper's dry clothes. The little girl was wearing another checked dress, but in different colors. She was very quiet, still upset by the loss of the doll.

Lemorne, already imagining himself in church attending her first communion, then as a witness at her wedding, refused to give his address. Seeing the disappointment on the face of Denise, his younger daughter, who probably thought she was missing out on a reward of millions, he smiled to himself. But he accepted the clothes as a gift, and the shopping net in which they'd put his own wet clothes.

They ambled on along the towpath in the pleasant

sunshine. His swimming adventure now seemed like a bit of good luck. Lemorne felt splendid in the new clothes that fit him to perfection, he enjoyed the silent admiration of his family which accompanied his every step, and he thought, I wonder if I could commit a *crime* too?

He imagined the most gruesome deed he could think of.

During the next three years not a day went by when he did not remember at least once the thought he'd had at the canal. Only then did he realize how different it was from his jump. He could stop halfway! Wasn't it true that having the idea obliged him to take at least the first step?

One day he filled in an order form at his school for calcium chloride. As he brought the envelope to the superintendent, he thought, The envelope is still in my hand.

When the calcium chloride arrived, he locked himself in the lab after school and, with the book by his side, set up the apparatus. From beneath the layer of foam that formed on the heated retort, the chloroform appeared drop by drop from the faucet, spreading a sickly sweet odor.

He repeated the procedure until he had one hundred milliliters, which he poured into a little brown bottle. He cleaned and tidied everything, and then he took the

bottle to his weekend cottage, a dilapidated place between Autun and Saulieu. He climbed the ladder to the
attic and put the bottle in a corner, amid dozens of odd
objects that probably had not been moved in a lifetime.
Christmas came, then New Year's. He spent two
weeks vacation with his family in Normandy.

The evening after their return, Lemorne drove to the
cottage again. He went to the attic and shined his flash-
light on the bottle. He gasped with awe and delight. It
was as if his fantasy were becoming palpable before his
eyes. Someone who would do the deed, to the very last
step, that he'd thought up along the canal would have
put that bottle here too.

There was no difference.

It was a game, unbelievably exciting.

The cottage, a disappointing inheritance of his wife's,
was twenty-six kilometers from Autun, on the outskirts
of a hamlet called Effours, on the local road, but isolated
and well out of sight. It consisted of three rooms and a
kitchen that looked out on its principal asset, an uneven
open meadow half the size of a football field, with an
ugly excavation that had once been intended as a swimming pool. The property was so well hidden by trees
along the roadside that it had even been ignored by
thieves; none of the possessions Lemorne had put there
had ever been stolen.

But gradually he had taken everything back home

again; nothing had come of his plans to make this a regular weekend retreat. Besides keeping out thieves, the trees also kept out much light, as did a hill covered with pine trees behind the house. The children thought the place was creepy. And so tableware, books, a Scrabble game had all been moved back to Autun. A tall, rusty rack with peeling paint and two hooks at the top stood in a corner of the meadow: a swing that had never done much swinging.

And tacked to a tree trunk, beside the dark entrance, a FOR SALE sign had been hanging for several years. It gave his telephone number, but no aspiring buyer had ever called.

He took down the sign and told his wife he wanted to take one last stab at making something out of the place. That was fine with her as long as she didn't have to help. Gabrielle, his older daughter, declared that she did want to help because she wanted to learn carpentry. Denise, his favorite, said she had absolutely no time for such things. Lemorne knew he could count on both of them being disinterested, but in Denise's eyes he saw thoughts of the mischievous parties she would be giving there one day.

On free afternoons and evenings, and on weekends, he now went to Effours. He bought a luggage rack and a small trailer to transport his supplies. It turned out that, as far as carpentry went, Gabrielle had imagined something quite different from the endless measuring and sanding of panels and getting her hands full of splinters, and she gave up after the first session. Lemorne repaired the shutters, threw out the animals and their nests, had the water and electricity reconnected, put in a refrigerator—enough to establish credibility without making the cottage attractive.

After endless bargaining at the flea market in Dole he bought an old single mattress for eighty francs. Carrying it on his head, he walked to his car. Hundreds of people could see him, did see him—and did not know what they saw: a step leading to a deeply shameful act. He felt delightfully evil, as if he had been drinking a potion that would make him invisible.

He went into the house and lay on the mattress, soaked a handkerchief with the chloroform, started his stopwatch, and sniffed. The afternoon in the lab filled him—he vanished. When he woke up, he was so dizzy and nauseated that it took him an eternity to remember his stopwatch. Eleven minutes had gone by. The man who would carry out the plan would have done this too.

His family came to inspect his progress. Lemorne smiled at their benevolent comments. They had a drink together sitting at a moldy table that he had found in the attic and put in the middle of the meadow. He knew what they were thinking: Daddy has gone crazy with his shack.

Denise discovered that the table had actually been some kind of bureau, for there was a drawer in it. She pulled it open and drew back with a scream; dozens of shiny red cockroaches squirmed inside it, feasting on the brownish remains of a field mouse.

"That was a nice scream," said Lemorne.

"Oh, I can do better than that," said Denise, already recovered from her fright.

"Really?"

"Yaheeh!"

"Wahooh," Lemorne screamed. "Let's see who can shout the loudest."

Gabrielle and his wife wouldn't play along, but laughed at the faces Denise made when she screamed.

The following evening Lemorne went to the nearest neighbor, a farmer across the road, from whom he sometimes bought eggs. They discussed the difficulty of keeping lonely houses from being robbed or vandalized.

"That reminds me," said Lemorne. "I was here yesterday evening with my family. I don't know if you saw us . . ." The farmer shook his head. "But just as we drove up we thought we heard someone screaming in our field. Did you hear anything, by any chance?"

The farmer had heard nothing.

In April, Lemorne read in the papers about a café in Lyon where an illegal weapons ring had been busted. A week later he went there and bought a gun. He put it in the attic, next to his bottle of chloroform.

• • •

How would the man, whose preparations he was copying step by step, get his victim into the house? To focus
his thoughts, Lemorne first decided *who* his victim
would be. From the very beginning he had known that
it would be a girl—perhaps because it was a little girl
he had rescued. But it should not be a child: It should
be someone completely aware of what was being done
to her.

A woman, then, but not an old one. Someone with a
lot to lose who would leave behind as much grief as
possible—a beautiful young woman would be ideal, a
mother preferably. Only then would this mind game of
his be worthwhile.

But as he shoveled and cemented, filling in the hole
of the swimming pool and working out the problem of
the abduction, he came to realize that this was only a
halfhearted approach. What was the point of following
these steps if it was already certain that he would not
take the last one?

Was that certain? Didn't the very question prove it
was *not* certain? He decided to leave that open for now.

Summer arrived, and Lemorne took some long drives
on the country roads in the Autun area. There were
plenty of hitchhikers, and quite often he saw girls alone.
But whenever he stopped, a young man would suddenly
pop up from behind a tree or a wall. Then Lemorne

would roll down his window and say, "You guys are cheaters, but I am not. I have enough room for two, but I only stopped for her." And he would continue on his way.

He never saw any girls who were really alone and eventually gave up on the idea of a hitchhiker. A prostitute? She would get in the car because of her profession, but the fact that prostitutes are predestined victims displeased him. Besides, the nature of their profession made them suspicious. They probably had their pimps or their colleagues take down the license-plate numbers of their clients.

One of his pupils or one of his daughters was out of the question. He couldn't imagine pulling that off without some evidence leading to him.

If he were to do it, the chloroform and the gun left only one problem: how to get his victim into the car.

He picked Denise up at the station. He held the door open for her, walked around the back of the car, got in, and reached behind her shoulders. Then he pushed the knob of her door lock down, suddenly curled his arm around her neck, and pinched her cheek.

"Why did you do that?"

"Because I love you."

"No, the lock."

"Didn't you read about that girl who fell out of a car on the highway because her door wasn't locked?"

"Really?"

"Well, she did. And I'm being careful about you all."

"Hey, Dad," said Denise. "Do you have a mistress? Oh, come on, don't look so shocked, a man your age has a perfect right to. Gaby never notices anything, but all that time you're supposed to be in that little house . . ."

"Your mother did notice that, didn't she?"

"What a giveaway!" Her eyes sparkled. "Do you really think she can't read the mileage? Come on, tell me! Does she live in Dijon?"

"My darling daughter," said Lemorne, "I prefer to be shocked."

He allowed a smile to come over his face, which, judging from Denise's expression, satisfied her.

Lemorne's car stood in the field in front of the cottage. He filled a small screw-top bottle with water and put it in the left pocket of his jacket. In the right-hand pocket he had a large handkerchief.

He opened the right-hand door, waited, and closed it. He walked around the back of the car, took the bottle out of his pocket, unscrewed the cap, and poured the water onto the handkerchief. Then he put the bottle back in his pocket, opened the other door, and sat down. Still holding the wet handkerchief in his right hand, he reached behind the passenger seat to the door lock and hooked his arm into a strong, tensed grip.

Ten or twenty times he filled the little bottle and started all over again, until the handkerchief left an irritating wet spot on his right hip.

It didn't go smoothly every time. He didn't get the water on the handkerchief fast enough, or he was still holding the bottle when he had to get into the car.

Just a matter of practice.

With twenty milliliters of chloroform in his bottle and the gun in his pocket, Lemorne drove to Dijon. He parked near the center of town in a wide, not-too-busy shopping street with trolley cars.

He waited for a woman walking alone. He took his pulse: 110.

In the side mirror, the reflection of a girl of about seventeen got larger. Dizzy with the beating of his heart, Lemorne got out of his car.

"Excuse me, can I ask you something?"

"Yes?"

"Could you tell me how to get to the main post office?"

"Are you driving?"

Lemorne nodded and she gave directions. He found them to be correct, and thanked her. He drove on a few blocks and asked a young woman who was walking alone where the post office was. She told him how to get there. By the time he had asked the fifth woman his pulse was down to seventy.

They all looked at him openly, and directed him to the post office in a friendly manner, though not always correctly. He told himself that the pleasant way in which he was helped was due to his own demeanor, often praised by his wife, and which had made him a popular and respected teacher in the school: ingratiating but never too familiar. Now and then, he had to suppress a desire to laugh: These women had no idea what they were being used for! They were training him!

"Excuse me, miss, could you tell me how to get to the main post office?"

"Oh, I just happen to be going there myself."

"Well, then, I've got my car. Can I give you a lift?"

They were standing right next to his car. He had already opened the door for her. This coincidence, which he'd been hoping, had not occurred until the sixth girl.

"Well . . ." she said, but a shadow filled her eyes, a hint of bitterness. "I'd rather walk."

"Right you are!" said Lemorne. "Such fine weather. *Merci!*"

He could see his mistake: The post office was the wrong choice for the young woman he had in mind. A department store would be more like it.

This became quite evident over the next few days, during his attempts in Beaune and Chalon. With chloroform and pistol in his pocket, he eventually began approaching his imagined victims without any emotion.

Several women happened to be on the way to the store he had asked for, but none of them got into his car. This was obviously not the right approach.

He then became aware of another, more serious flaw. If he kept addressing only Frenchwomen, and always in the same part of the country, he was unnecessarily increasing the risk that these witnesses of his failed attempts would eventually read about the successful one in the papers. With foreign women, the recollection of a man who had tried to lure them into a car would be scattered all over Europe! The *Progrès de Lyon* wasn't read in Uppsala! But how could he approach foreign women? Very simple. The Autoroute ran very close to Autun. And suddenly Lemorne saw the elegance of this solution: He would not only find thousands of foreign women at the gas stations there, different ones every hour, but they would be instantly recognizable as such by the license plates of their cars.

The exam period was over, the school year had come to an end. Lemorne had two weeks to himself before leaving for vacation. He bought a pass for the Autoroute, and spent a whole day near the coffee machines of gas stations, observing the routine.

Soon a pattern emerged. The man drove. While he had the tank filled, the woman went to the ladies' room. After that she had a look in the store. The man, in the meantime, would finish at the gas pump and park the car in the lot near the service station. He did not go in. When the woman was finished inside the store she walked out to him. She was temporarily isolated.

But how to get her into the car? An image came up: A few weeks ago a woman, totally unknown to him, *had* been inside his car. He hadn't thought anything of it because it had been connected with her job—but had that been all?

When he was picking up lumber he had ordered in Moulins, none of the regular employees had been available. The receptionist had jumped into the car with him, accompanied him to the warehouse, and helped him secure the lumber to his roof rack. She was not a particularly athletic or sturdy-looking woman, but she had enjoyed doing it, as if she had been *waiting* for such a chore.

Just because she was a woman? Women don't usually lug things around—was that what made it fun? Women don't usually do carpentry—was that why Gabrielle had wanted to try it?

And even if she would not enjoy it, wouldn't a demand on her physical strength throw a woman off?—distract her from her usual wariness when facing an unknown man?

A young Englishwoman with a package of sausages in her hands seemed lost in thought.

"Excuse me, but could you possibly help me out?"

He had to repeat his question. She did not speak French.

"Could you possibly help me?" he said in English. "I have to couple my trailer to the car." The word *trailer* was correct; but to connect it to the car he chose *couple*, taking a gamble, for the dictionary also listed *hitch* and *join.*

"I? My husband . . ." Her eyes searched outside, where her camper no longer stood. She shrugged her shoulders with a laugh. This was the reaction he had expected: surprise.

"It only takes a minute. Would you do that?" He asked the question in the same way that he would ask his students to fetch some fresh chalk, and as if she had already agreed, he walked to the exit. He did not check to see if she was following him. No one would think of them as belonging together, and she'd never have a chance to shake him off with a polite excuse. Would she put the sausages back, or would she stop at the counter to pay for them first? That had been a mistake. He should have addressed her before she had picked up something.

He stopped at the passenger door of his car, which was parked along the sidewalk behind the store, and a few feet behind him the girl stopped. She did not have the sausages with her, and she looked about her as if searching for something.

"So where is your trailer?"

"Oh," Lemorne laughed. "I should have told you. It's over there." He pointed to the larger parking lot, some hundred yards farther on, where his trailer stood propped up. "Do you mind walking there?"

He took a step toward the other side of the car, then stopped and smiled. "Or, why not get in, that's easier." He returned to the passenger side and held the door open for her.

A dark veil passed over her eyes, the way a cloud suddenly passes across a sunny swimming pool. For a moment she seemed undecided.

"I'll just walk," she said absently.

"As you like," said Lemorne.

He drove to the trailer, and instead of the girl, a tired-looking young man appeared who helped him with surly suspicion. Rightly so, for although there were four hundred pounds of rubble in the trailer, there was really no need for help. Had the girl already sensed that he didn't need her assistance when he pointed the trailer out to her?

After various attempts, of which he kept notes in order not to go back to the same gas station too soon, Lemorne stopped. Basically the method he had chosen was good; the women he approached had been taken by surprise, and most of them did follow him to his car. But each time he pointed to his trailer and suggested they get into his car a dark expression settled on their faces, and without exception they had managed to stop being polite. They walked, called their boyfriends, or left him standing there.

So, now what? A sailboat in tow? A camper? Where would he leave them? Wouldn't his family, his neighbors, the inhabitants of Effours raise their eyebrows? No, whatever he did should remain invisible, like a brick in a wall.

It was Lemorne's birthday: He was forty-one. His wife gave him a sweater with a matching shirt, a pair of blue-striped underpants, and a coffeemaker for the cottage. From Gabrielle he received a tie and a magnifying glass that could also be used as a paperweight. From Denise he got a bunch of flowers, a box of honey wafers, a key chain with a metal *R* attached, and a surprise. With old pieces of Lego she had built a house, whose chimney turned out to be the cap of an eight-color pencil. In front of it stood a little plastic man holding a hammer. That was him, and the house was the cottage.

Lemorne could see how the little man would be squashed by the pen if he tried to write with it, and he burst out laughing. Suddenly, cold shivers ran through his body. He had seen the solution.

It wasn't the trailer that should be heavier; *he* should be weaker. He must go back to his jump.

Once, long ago, he had been weak. People had

opened doors for him, carried his bag; strangers had fought to pick up his books if he dropped them.

That was when his leg had been in a cast and his arm in a sling.

The next morning Lemorne drove 150 kilometers to Lyon. He bought a sling for his arm at a drugstore, tied it around his neck in a dark underground parking garage, and went out on the street wearing it. He had an erection; he felt like a king, as if in the first flush of drunkenness on first-class wine.

He bought two pounds of apples and had them put in a plastic bag; with the bag in one hand, the other in the sling, he spent the whole afternoon walking in and out of hotel lobbies, movie theaters, cafés, and everywhere people appeared and held doors open for him. The handicapped are helpless! They have to be assisted! He walked about the city for hours, sometimes afraid he would burst into uncontrollable laughter in the middle of a crowded boulevard: People saw him without knowing what they were really seeing—the answer to a riddle that had not yet begun!

"Excuse me, miss. Could you help me out?"

The girl looked at his sling. "That depends," she said. She spoke very good French for a Dutch girl.

"I have to hitch my *remorque* to my car. It's difficult with this thing."

"A *remorque?*"

"My trailer. Little trailer," he said in English.

She bit her lip, and looked over to where her boy-friend had just pulled away from the pump.

"I'm not strong," she said.

"Oh, you'll manage," laughed Lemorne. "Won't you help?"

Hesitantly she raised her shoulders.

"Merci," said Lemorne, and walked out. She followed; he congratulated himself for having foreseen the success of this surprise attack. There was no sign that she thought it strange that he would be driving with his arm in a sling.

They stood near his car; the girl looked around.

"Where is it?" she asked.

Lemorne pointed. "Over there. I suppose I should have told you. I'll drive, if you'll . . ."

Her face went blank, a darkness flitted across it, then disappeared.

"I'll just get in, then," she said reluctantly. She opened the door and sat down.

Lemorne walked around the car, reached with his right hand inside the sling, and heard a scream, followed by the sound of screeching tires and a dull thump.

A body tumbled through the air. It landed with a thud in an unnatural position. People came running from all sides, creating a multicolored curtain that blocked his view. The girl got out, said something to him that he did not understand, and ran toward the crowd.

A few moments later Lemorne saw her with a man, standing hand in hand near the accident.

Fate, he thought, and drove away.

On his way to Autun he stopped at Effours to drop off a box of tiles he had bought earlier that day.

He drove onto his lawn, and saw an orange tent half set up. Two boys were lying in the grass and jumped up in a fright. They turned out to be two German hitchhikers, boys of about seventeen who spoke no French. Lemorne had to resort to his rusty German. They had been taken off guard by his sudden appearance and seemed ill at ease. It had been too late for them to reach a camping ground, they said, and they had hoped to spend the night here.

They had been there for half an hour. No, no one had told them they could set up their tent here. They had tried to get another lift; they had spoken to no one. They had simply been dropped off in the village and had walked up here. If Lemorne would let them stay, they would leave as early as possible tomorrow morning.

"All right then, you can stay," said Lemorne.

He sat in his car and thought. The boys observed him through the windshield, not quite sure whether they dared to smile. Lemorne took the gun out of the glove compartment and got out. He chose one of the boys to be the first and shot him dead. He would have shot the second one immediately after, but was mesmerized by the way his lower lip dropped away from his little mustache, and it took several seconds before he shot again.

He packed the bodies into his car and took down the tent. He cursed the boys because he had to pull all the pegs out of the ground.

When the tent was also loaded into the car, he walked across the road to buy a dozen eggs from the farmer. The conversation turned to holiday traffic in general, and hitchhikers in particular.

"There are quite a few this year," said Lemorne.

"You even see them around here," said the farmer. "Two of them were standing by your driveway about an hour ago."

"Really? I didn't see anything."

"They must have gotten a ride."

"I never pick up hitchhikers," said Lemorne.

The farmer shrugged. "I do sometimes," he said.

His pass for the Autoroute came in handy now, and Lemorne drove south until nightfall. Somewhere in the mountains between Lyon and Saint-Étienne he dumped the bodies and the tent into a ravine along a side road.

He drove home and wondered whether or not he would continue to follow in the footsteps of the man who would go all the way. Almost four years had passed since that moment at the Canal de Bourgogne, and one year since he had ordered the calcium chloride—and he still didn't know!

When he got home and took the eggs from the backseat, he saw that he had forgotten to put the box of tiles in the cottage.

The next day was clear and glorious, and Lemorne suggested a swim. His wife did not want to go, so he drove with Gabrielle and Denise to a little lake a few kilometers from Autun. It was crowded, and among the strangely truncated statues on the water's surface he reconized various pupils.

Spurs from the hills and giant tree roots divided the sloping embankment into dozens of tiny beaches. Because they arrived rather late, Lemorne and his daughters had to settle for one of the smallest, but for some reason, more and more boys happened to emerge from the water or descend from the hill to sit near them. His own pupils greeted him politely, and they stayed to sit and chat with Gabrielle and Denise or with each other.

Lemorne read the newspaper and found an account of the accident he had witnessed at the gas station. The victim turned out to have been a twenty-one-year-old Englishman, L. Bodding, from Hull, who had come off reasonably lightly with a slight concussion and a broken leg.

His little section of beach was getting crowded. Twice Lemorne had to move farther toward the edge.

There were at least twelve boys sitting there now, and still only two girls: his daughters.

Lemorne stood up, cleared his throat, and asked for attention.

"Ladies and gentlemen," he said. "I have two announcements to make. First of all, I noticed that several of you have cigarettes with you. Some of you have even tried to light one on the sly. That's not necessary. We're on vacation, and for those of you who are my pupils, this means that school rules are on vacation too. Second"—he paused for some cheers—"I'm treating you all to ice cream. But I'm not as nice as I seem, for I have no intention of walking up the hill and getting it myself."

He held out a hundred-franc note, there was a burst of hurrahs, and five minutes later everyone had an ice cream.

At one o'clock Lemorne left. Gabrielle and Denise wanted to stay, and after having promised him that they'd be home on time, he gave them some money for snacks and the bus.

Lemorne had lunch with his wife, helped her pack for the vacation they were to take four days later, slept an hour, and at five o'clock drove toward the Autoroute.

He unhitched his little trailer in the large parking lot near the grass, then drove back and parked his car along the sidewalk behind the store. He uncorked his bottle of chloroform and plugged it with a rag. He hung the sling around his neck, put his left arm in, and slipped the little bottle inside, bottom first.

He stepped out and inhaled the delicious early evening air, prickly with the fumes of exhaust. This was the smell of travel and expectation; he had come to feel at home in these service areas, these constantly renewing villages where one could explore many different countries at once.

He walked to the end of the lawn, enjoying the looks that his sling got from the people resting and playing ball on the grass.

The long-legged girl pulled two cans of Coca-Cola out of the vending machine.

"Please excuse me," said Lemorne. "Could you possibly give me a hand? I have this little trailer that I want to hitch to my car, and it's hard to do with this." He held up his arm in the sling. That sling was really a find—her reserve faded even before her gaze left his arm.

"Me? Sure, *naturellement.*" She pronounced the last syllable with a friendly lift. "Broken?"

"Yes, playing tennis." He mimicked a forehand with his right arm. "Slipped and . . . bonk, broke an arm."

"That's rough," said the girl.

"You'll give me a hand?"

He already had walked on and she followed him.

"So, where is your trailer?"

"Oh, over there," said Lemorne. "Sorry about that, I

should have told you. Now you'll have to walk all the way."

"That's nothing."

"Yes . . . or else I can drive you. I have to go there too, after all." He laughed and held the door open.

"Okay, that'll be quicker," said the girl, but her voice had suddenly become toneless and she stood still.

"Get in," said Lemorne.

She clutched the cans of Coke and the same dark cloud that he had observed over and over again when he asked a woman to get in passed over her face.

"I don't know," she said to herself, almost inaudibly, as if she were thinking about something else. "Maybe I'll just walk."

Together they hitched up Lemorne's trailer. With his right arm he did the heavy work, while she made sure that the claw of the shaft landed right on the ball bearing of the hitch.

He followed her with his eyes until she reached her car. She said something to her boyfriend, after which both of them looked back in his direction.

"Merci!" Lemorne shouted, and waved at them.

He got in, waited until they had driven away, and took off his sling. In his notebook he wrote: *Mobil "Le Chien Blanc": 28.7.75; 6:00–6:15 P.M.*

After consulting his previous notes he decided he could safely make another attempt two stations farther on.

• • •

A girl of about twenty-five, who reminded him of Denise, got out of a car with Dutch plates. Lemorne stood by the coffee-vending machine and watched her walk right past him on her way to the corridor where the rest rooms were.

It was a bit after seven o'clock but the station was still so crowded that there was a waiting line at all the gas pumps. This made it less likely that her boyfriend would be finished before she left the store.

Tired of the endless waiting by vending machines, Lemorne went outside. He stood near the doors and watched the Dutch car inch its way toward the pump. Would the girl stay long enough in the ladies' room? If she was anything like Gabrielle and Denise, there was a good chance. Suddenly he noticed that a man was going to take a photograph of two small children standing right next to him in front of the door, and he stepped aside.

The Dutchman paid the attendant, and Lemorne went back in. Right inside the glass doors he passed the girl who looked like Denise.

He walked over to the coffee machine and started searching for another suitable victim. Ten, twenty women walked past his critical eye toward the restroom. He rejected them, and a moment later they were outside again with cups of coffee or cans of soda in their hands, unaware that they had just lived through the most important moment in their lives.

He spoke to a Belgian woman, but she pretended not to hear him, an unusual reaction. Lemorne got thirsty and put two francs into the soda machine. He tried to wrestle the Schweppes can out of the slot with his right hand alone, but it was very awkward with that damn sling. It was a situation, as he had noticed before, that worked like a pot of honey on flies. But he could not be selective this way and it was a German in his sixties who fell into the unintentional trap. He told Lemorne that he had fallen out of a tree at the age of eleven. He extricated Lemorne's can and opened it for him, wishing him a speedy recovery.

Lemorne drank, threw the empty can into the trash bin, and decided to leave. It wouldn't do to hang around in the same place for too long.

He returned to his car, took off his sling, and wrote in his notebook: *TOTAL "Venoy-Grosse-Pierre": 28.7.75, 7:00–7:20 P.M.*

He hooked up his trailer, looking out over the lawn where people were kicking a ball around, sat leaning against the fence, or were simply stretched out on the grass.

As he started the car he saw from the fuel gauge that he needed gas. He drove back to the pumps, where there were still long lines of cars. The cold tonic had already reached his bladder, and after having paid, he parked near the store, next to a large trailer truck.

When he came out of the bathroom, he saw the girl

who had escaped him before, the Dutch girl who looked a little like Denise. She stood in the back of the store, near the soda machines, alone.

Although he was unprepared for the situation, Lemorne went back to the coffee machine. He slipped two franc pieces into the slot and pushed the button for black coffee with sugar. While the coffee splattered into his cup, the girl was rummaging in her purse. She was making it unnecessarily complicated, for she kept clutching a bunch of keys.

She looked at him and took a step in his direction.

"Pardon," she said. "Do you speak French?"

"I *am* French," said Lemorne.

"I miss one franc for the machine. Can you change, please?" Her French was halting, but a bit passable.

"Let me see if I can help you," said Lemorne. He took his wallet out of his pocket. Her smallest coin was a ten-franc piece, which he could not change; their vain attempts to work it out made them laugh.

She went to the cashier and changed it there.

Lemorne took another sip of his coffee. "Let's go," he said to himself. He took his car keys out of his pocket and played with them absentmindedly.

The girl returned and pulled out a can of Fanta and a beer. She gave Lemorne a smile. It almost seemed as if she were looking at his sling, and yet he was no longer wearing it!

Lemorne clicked his tongue. He could not think of anything to say.

The girl took a step toward him.

"Can I have a look?" she said.

"What do you mean?"

She pointed to the car keys in his hand.

"How nice!" she said, pointing at the *R* dangling from his key chain. "Do you know where I can buy one?"

Lemorne thought. He smiled and shrugged his shoulders. "I'm a salesman for these things," he said, wondering whether she would understand the French word *réprésentant* for salesman. "I deal in them, I've got a whole carful."

"Really?" An idea came to her mind. "Can I perhaps buy one from you? Also with an *R*?"

He looked at her and sighed. "Why not."

"Yes? How much is it?"

"Nine francs fifty," said Lemorne.

He emptied his cup, threw it in the trash bin, and motioned for her to follow him. He heard her footsteps behind him.

He stopped at his car door, and she paused alongside the trailer, obviously thinking that the key chains were in there.

"No, no," said Lemorne, and he pointed at the backseat, where the box of tiles still stood. "J. J. MONTMÉJEAN–AUTUN–TUILIER," it said. The arm sling lay against it with the little bottle peeking out of one of its folds.

They stood next to each other. To their left was the big truck, a camper had pulled up on their right; his car seemed to be parked in a narrow alley.

Lemorne opened his door, leaned over toward the backseat, and straightened up again. "It's rather heavy," he said, pointing at the box. "The easiest would be if you got in for a moment."

He gestured toward the other door. And in her face too, he saw that dark shadow, that glimmer of mistrust.

"An *R*?" said Lemorne.

"Yes." She began to walk around, holding her cans. He reached into the backseat; before she got to her door he had already inverted the bottle and had the wet rag in his hand.

She sat down and turned toward the box.

"Excuse me just a moment," said Lemorne and reached around behind her. With a wild gasp she turned away from him; Lemorne bent his arm and covered her face with his hand, tensed and forceful.

She arched her back like a high diver about to take the plunge. Then she let her drinks drop and slid down into the seat.

Gotcha, thought Lemorne.

He started the car and drove out of the parking lot, onto the Autoroute du Soleil.

4

Nothing could possibly have arrived on the first day, but Rex went to check anyway, on foot, and without an umbrella, in spite of the drizzle. It was a ritual, something you did on your own power, without anything between you and heaven.

He lived in an apartment building on the outskirts of Amsterdam, just across the canal that had marked the border of the city at the time of his birth. His walk led him along a wide boulevard of a tranquillity that had surely not been intended by the city planners, and past the spot where as a child he had watched the launching of a hot-air-balloon race. Later, the school from which he had graduated, more than twenty years ago, had been built on that same spot.

He crossed the bridge to a peaceful neighborhood with expensive apartment buildings, where the only cars were the parked ones. On one of these streets was the post office, with a separate entrance to the private mailboxes.

Rex's box was at eye level, but once it was open, he still reached into it all the way.

It was empty, and he walked back. It was a nice walk, not more than a half hour all told, and he decided to walk the following days, too.

Back at work, as he got up from his desk every now and again to stare out the window, he suddenly noticed something that made him blink. A large yellow station wagon that hadn't been washed in ages was parked right below his window, and in the grime on the hood someone had written: "REX I LOVE YOU SANDRA."

My God, thought Rex. The first message is from her.

It was a very unusual car, and he had never seen it before. He moved to the edge of his window until he could see the license number; it was an ordinary Dutch one.

He didn't feel a cold shiver, though he would have welcomed one; after eight years he had become used to such coincidences. Once, when he was traveling through the region that had been his and Saskia's destination when she vanished, many walls along the road were painted white, with a large red question mark in the middle and some numbers, always the same ones: 75.07.29, with periods in between, as if someone wanted to make sure they would be read as a date. It differed only by one day from that of her disappearance—it had been the telephone number of the advertising agency that leased the walls.

There had once been a mouse that stood with its paws against the display window of a pet shop, looking at him for so long and with such intensity that Rex had been painfully sure that Saskia was looking at him through those eyes.

But when you began to see the world this way, such messages were everywhere. The mileage on the odometer at the TOTAL station, the dates of their births, their meeting, her disappearance resurfaced constantly in his life, only slightly disguised: The wedding announcement of a certain Rex and Saskia appeared in the papers; he had a vivid dream about the son of some vague acquaintances and discovered he had been born on the day that Saskia had disappeared.

Dearer to him than any of these messages, except for his dream about the golden egg, was a large wooden clothespin, the last relic of Saskia's contribution to his housekeeping, and which he still used as she had intended: to reseal bags of potato chips that had been opened.

Rex went on working, and when he looked at the car later that day, he discovered something he had overlooked before. Also written on the hood was: "WRITING THIS WILL SCRATCH THE BLISS."

Jesus, he thought. What a great sentence. Tears came to his eyes. Had anyone ever had such a great love letter parked right under his window? This was a supreme, poetic truth: The expression of love destroys it. Regardless of Saskia and any communications she might be trying to send from wherever she was, Rex had immediately fallen in love with this Sandra.

But who was she? He knew no one by that name. Was she one of those frustrated women in their thirties who, like him, were alone in their apartments all day? Wouldn't they be more likely to agree to some quick sex with a stranger than to write poetry on the hood of a car?

Could it be that girl of about fifteen whom he saw now and then in the hallway, and whom he had secretly nicknamed "the giggler"? Once when he met her on the street, accompanied by a girlfriend, she turned her face away, making it clear that he'd been on her mind.

How would she, whoever she was, know that his name was Rex? On his door it said "R. Hofman." Was this message really intended for him? Perhaps it was destined for a Rex living in Utrecht, with the car creating confusion all over the country wherever Rexes lived. But there weren't that many Rexes. And the message was recent, for no new grime covered it.

Suddenly Rex was overcome by a powerful and physical longing for this Sandra. Should he write "OK DROP BY" on the hood of the car? But what if it was that schoolgirl, and her parents saw him do it? No: *She* knew who *he* was, not the other way around—if she had something in mind, let her take the next step.

In any case, his day was made, and Rex cheerfully

went back to the article he was writing for a popular science magazine on Cantor, the nineteenth-century German mathematician.

Every now and then he checked to see whether the yellow car was still there, and as a joke he wrote on the "women's" page in his datebook, in the section "Poss. Prosp.": Sandra.

On the second day there was nothing in his mailbox.

On the third day there were three letters. One of these, in a childish handwriting, was signed "Sakia." How annoying, this French disregard for the spelling of foreign names. It was an eight-page letter and began with a pornographic account of Sakia's experiences in a brothel. Rex did not finish it. The second one was from a clairvoyant in Autun, who predicted that he would see Saskia within a few days. Rex knew that Autun was not far from the TOTAL station where Saskia had disappeared, and looked it up on the map: eighty kilometers. He put this letter aside. The third one was from the magazine *Photo-Vie,* offering him five thousand francs for the story if he found Saskia again. Rex answered that they could have such a story for free on the condition that they publish a story about her disappearance now, with photographs.

The yellow car was still there.

But suddenly Rex saw that he had read the second

message wrong. It really said: "WRITING THIS WILL SCRATCH THE POLISH." Upon closer scrutiny, the handwriting was also different from Sandra's "REX I LOVE YOU," and a new layer of dust had covered it, as if it had been written earlier. Probably these two messages did not belong together.

So Sandra was less poetic than he had thought, which nevertheless did not wipe out her declaration of love.

Someone from an Amsterdam newspaper called him for an interview about his French advertising campaign. Rex was as elaborate as possible in his answers, but refused to say how much it had cost him.

Lieneke called to find out whether he was the one who had rung her doorbell just as she was coming out of the shower, but who had gone by the time she opened the door. After a few words it became clear that she wanted to see him sooner. After their sad drive home from vacation they had seen each other only once, a few days ago, by chance, in the university library. They had made a date for two weeks later. She sounded depressed, which upset Rex. She came over that same evening and they had a long and tender, almost loving conversation. She stayed the night.

On the fourth day, a Thursday, the yellow car was still there, in the same spot below his window.

Lieneke had come on her bicycle, and now she walked with him to the post office. In the windy parking lot they encountered the young girl from the hall who might be Sandra. Rex stared hard at her and she looked back. He was amazed to see how pretty she was, and she was certainly not fifteen. He must have thought that years ago and never updated it.

She did not show any reaction. In case she was indeed Sandra, Rex was a little embarrassed at having Lieneke along.

He took her for a cup of coffee in the coffee shop and bought the newspaper. The interview was printed on page two, with a much reduced reproduction of his French ad and a photograph of Saskia that covered three columns. As so often before, he felt that series of impulses in his brain: What a beautiful woman—Saskia!—she's gone.

It was the same photograph that had been in all the papers eight years ago and that he now used again in his ads: the one he had taken on the café terrace in Paris on the morning before she disappeared, the last picture of her. In seven-eighths profile, she looked at Rex with a knowing smile, as if she had something up her sleeve. The caption read: . . . *two cans* . . .

Under the title "French Appeal for Missing Girlfriend," the story of her disappearance was told once more, abbreviated, and with a few small errors. They'd gone ahead and quoted the sum he'd supposedly paid for the ads: *The price: a cool eighty thousand guilders. He must have gone deep into dept for this. Hoping for what?* "*Nothing," says Hofman. "It's a tribute.*"

He showed Lieneke the article. When she had read it she nodded without comment, and Rex realized how rude he had been to buy the paper in her presence.

They said good-bye, and Rex went to his post office box, which this time contained seventeen letters from France.

When he got home he opened his datebook to the women's page. To the two names under the heading "Available" he added: Lieneke. In the "Poss. Prosp." section he crossed out Sandra and instead wrote:

Hallway Sandra
Car Hood Sandra
(Same?)

On a slip of paper he wrote the names Saskia and Sandra underneath each other. Both names had the same number of letters. If the identical letters were removed, the letters NDR and SKI remained.

Rex examined them for a while, and wrote: DR. NIKS. Then, KIND R & S.

He read his mail from France, which included two more letters from magazines. They made the same offer as *Photo-Vie* and Rex sent them the same answer.

Quite a few writers claimed to have seen Saskia somewhere recently and Rex wondered if he owed all of them a thank-you note: Without identification these communications were worthless. One letter mentioned a pharmacy in Avallon where Saskia was supposedly working as an assistant. Avallon was just ten kilometers from the TOTAL station and he wrote to the pharmacy asking for further information and a photograph of the assistant.

A few clairvoyants and private detectives offered their services by sending him their publicity material. A woman from Fontainebleau wrote to say that she had once been followed for days by a man in a car who kept calling out, "Come on, pussy."

There was also a letter from the driver of the Amaddei Frères truck, whom Rex had met eight years before during the police investigation. He wrote that he was well, inquired after Rex's health, and wished him success with his search.

Rex took out his photograph of the truck once more. According to the official reconstruction it could indeed have been taken the moment Saskia came out with the cold drinks. The door of the station was not visible: It had been precisely hidden by the cab of the truck.

A distant memory that always embarrassed Rex a bit resurfaced from his childhood. A new liquid had been described on a children's radio show: If sprinkled over a photograph it would allow you to see what had happened a second later. The first hundred kids to respond would get a free bottle. He had been nine years old at the time, and had immediately mailed in a card, only to receive a reply saying that it had been an April Fools' joke, and that the show would appreciate it if he'd join their fan club.

Then, for the thousandth time, Rex examined the

only other photograph that had come to light as a result
of his search: two kids wearing RICARD caps, and
dimly, leaning over the back of his car, himself.

He pushed away the pictures and stared at the letters
NDR and SKI on his pad. One could also make
DRINKS out of them.

Suddenly he felt an unpleasant premonition and
went to his window. It turned out to be true: The yellow
station wagon was no longer there. Rex slipped on his
coat and searched the parking lots of all the apartment
buildings in the neighborhood, but the car was really
gone. He blamed himself for not having taken down the
license number—an inexplicable and irreparable over-
sight.

This discovery depressed him, and he knew that he
would not be able to get any more work done. Cantor
would just have to wait. He'd have liked to call Lieneke
right away, but that would have been taking advantage
of her, so soon after their meeting again. He had no
desire to see either of the two other women on his
"Available" list.

Later that evening he called one of them.

As soon as he was alone again the next morning, he
wrote Lieneke a letter. He allowed his melancholy free
rein without proposing anything concrete.

Having dropped it in the mailbox at his post office, he
walked to the side entrance to collect his own mail,

when a man came toward him, one hand half-raised, and looked straight at him. He was a man of about fifty, tall and well groomed, pleasant-looking and at the same time imposing. His blond, graying hair was cut short and he wore a neatly pressed beige raincoat: the prototype of an American presidential candidate on the campaign trail.

Rex's heart began to pound wildly, just as it had when he'd watched a real execution on film.

And then he recognized him.

It was the man with the sling.

"Are you Rex Hofman?" the man asked.

"Yes," said Rex.

"Do you speak French?"

"Yes."

"Raymond Lemorne," he said. "I saw your ad in the paper." He held out his hand and, impressed that this man was a participant in his adventure, Rex shook it—the contact sent a bolt of electricity through his arm. Eight years ago he hadn't seen him for more than a few seconds, but the tip of his sling, poking into the RI-CARD kids' picture like a curious white nose, had etched the man's face into his memory forever.

Yes, of course, the arm would be healed by now. Why had this man come, why hadn't he written a letter like all the others?

"Do you know something about her?"

"Yes."

She too had heard this voice. It almost sounded as if he had brought her along, as if they would now go to a restaurant where Saskia was waiting for him. She was in black, as if to apologize for all the irreparably lost years, and she had definitely aged: she was a lady of thirty-three, but she had also remained that wanton sex bomb. She was cheerful and warm, glad to see him, and she had brought him a bottle of exotic liqueur, lousy stuff of course, but lovingly chosen for its beautiful label . . .

"I want to talk in my car," said the man.

"Is she dead?" Rex heard himself say *mort* instead of *morte*, as if correct grammar would be disrespectful.

Lemorne made a gesture with his hand and led him to a car with a French license plate, parked in front of the post office. He opened the door for Rex, walked around, and then climbed in himself.

"Is she dead?"

"Yes."

"Yes," said Rex.

The man looked ahead theatrically, his arms braced against the wheel, with an expression he might have practiced in the mirror—in the same way that everything he said sounded like a part he had learned by heart. A fear that had been growing in Rex over the last few years suddenly disappeared; the fear that the kidnapper himself might be dead, and that the riddle would remain unsolved forever.

From very far away, as far as the garbage truck that

stood in front of them, where two young men were tossing in bags with slow, graceful swoops, came the notion that he ought to punch this man in the nose. But this would make no sense. This was an emissary of Saskia's, the highest authority he had ever met.

Without asking Rex, Lemorne started the car and drove off.

"Where are we going?" asked Rex. "I have to pick up some mail here."

"I want to talk to you in a quiet place. I'll bring you back later if that's what you want."

He drove regally, smoothly, shifting without a hitch, with scientifically accurate turns at the curves. Rex was crushed by his presence. They drove past his own building to a parking lot along a ditch, across from a complex of tennis courts without nets.

Lemorne opened his side window a crack, reached into the pocket of his raincoat, and held up a bunch of keys. Rex recognized them as the keys from back then, with the stringy leather strap.

This is going so fast, he thought. This has to slow down.

"I can't give them to you," said Lemorne. "I'm sure you'll understand." He put them back in his pocket.

"What happened to her?"

"I've come here to let you know. But there is only one way that I can do it. By having you undergo the same thing."

Someone was scraping together the dead leaves on the tennis courts with a kind of broom with long, curved teeth, like a beggar's hand.

"Then I'll die," said Rex.

"Yes."

"You're crazy."

"That is irrelevant," said Lemorne.

They were silent for a while. Then, abruptly, as if he had looked up in a book how long it would take someone to digest this sort of thing, Lemorne continued.

"I cannot communicate this to you in any other way. I want to keep living my life as it is now. You may leave and take down my license number, and I did give you my real name, by the way. But I assure you that there is absolutely no evidence against me, no one would be able to find any clues, and I'd remain silent forever. The risk I am running is something different. You can kill me. I admit your right to do so. But your advertisement has convinced me that you will do anything to know what happened, so I've decided to give you this chance. If you do not follow my instructions exactly, that will be the end of my offer. I am now returning to France, with or without you. This is your only chance. I'll give you five minutes to decide."

"I'm coming," said Rex.

"Do you have your passport?"

"Yes."

"Good." He buckled his seat belt and drove off.

• • •

Motionless, his arms stretched out like a statue of a coachman, and equally silent, Lemorne drove south. His car held the road smoothly, the speedometer hovering at 140 kilometers an hour was the only sign that they were moving at all.

Night fell.

So here he was, this man about whom he had been thinking all these years without knowing what he looked like. Every now and then Lemorne took a wafer-like cookie from a box on the dashboard and ate it with a crunching sound, his lips and nose the only parts of his face that moved.

Rex smoked. He had traveled this road too often to still think of it as the road from back then. But suddenly at an overpass just outside of Roubaix a memory that had been waiting for this particular trip surfaced unexpectedly. Here they had played Animals with *K*, and she had insisted for a long time, perhaps causing the first irritation of the day, that her *"Klarion"* really existed. "You eat it at Christmastime. It's a kind of turkey!"

Lemorne had given him five minutes to make up his mind, but of course that was nonsense. He had hours; he could get out of the car at a gas station, or at any tollbooth on the turnpike. He could still do it. Was Lemorne bluffing? He had those keys. Could they prove anything if Rex took them away from him? Maybe that he had done *something*, but not *what*. Or would the

simplest investigation reveal what he had done with
Saskia? Perhaps not—and if Lemorne did not speak, he
would have missed his only chance to find out.

He had to think.

Time was of the essence now; they had already
passed Paris. But he couldn't seem to summon up the
strength to think clearly. Only one thing counted: to
know what had happened to Saskia. Knowing would
coincide with the destruction of the one who knew—
but this was beautiful in a way. Sandra had already
prepared him for it: Writing this will scratch the bliss.

Now and then he ate something out of a box that
Lemorne had put beside him. It contained four sand-
wiches wrapped in plastic—two with cold cuts and two
with cheese, all four with a leaf of lettuce—two small
pieces of packaged soft cheese, a container of mustard,
two packs of juice, straws, a tangerine, one Golden
Delicious apple, a chocolate bar, and paper napkins.
How sick would a mind have to be, to assemble a picnic
like that for such a trip? And how sick was his own
mind, to be feeling this slight but undeniable resent-
ment that Lemorne had those wafers and he did not?

Rex remembered a magazine article he had once
written about falling, for which he had used interviews
with people who had survived falling from airplanes.
None of them had been afraid. They had been resigned,
curious, and especially lucid.

And that was how he felt now: brilliantly lucid. A

kind of peace filled him, along with a feeling of comple-
tion that he remembered from long ago, when he used
to write poetry. There had been rare moments when
purpose or success or even beauty or meaning seemed
irrelevant, and only the exciting awareness remained
that he was imitating something, that he was finally
doing what something very high up wanted him to do,
and that it was his responsibility to keep doing it step-
by-step.

The autoroute began to take on the shape it had in
the riddle of Saskia.

There was the sign: TOTAL, 900 METERS; and at the top
of the slope, the lights of the gas station. Rex had not
been back there since the investigation. He had driven
by, but had always looked straight ahead.

Lemorne slowed down and drove behind the station
to the big parking lot near the field. He stopped at the
end. No one was there. They got out, and from the back
of the car Lemorne produced a thermos bottle deco-
rated with flowers.

Rex realized that he had had the underlying thought
that somehow he would find a way out of this. But how?
He was now afraid. He recognized everything. He
sniffed the cool evening air and, forgetting Lemorne for
a moment, walked onto the field. The small hill without
a babbling mountain stream was still there. He climbed
it and looked back at the service station and the pumps,

and at the Milky Way of garbage that littered the grass
in precisely the same way as it had on that night, as if
year in and year out someone saw to it that the right
amount of trash was always here.

He turned aside. Lemorne stood behind him at the
foot of the hill. In one hand he held the thermos bottle;
with the other he handed Rex a plastic cup.

"Drink," he said.

A great, simple fear unfolded in Rex's belly. He was
confused—no doubt he would be tortured. How many
seconds did he have left to calculate whether Lemorne
could be forced to reveal his secret some other way?

"What's in it?"

"A soporific. It will take effect in fifteen minutes,
during which time I will tell you the beginning. Drink
it.

"Drink!" said Lemorne.

There was a dreadful fear—that Lemorne would
leave. Rex looked at the cup in his hand. He would set
it to his lips, but now it was still in his hand. It was
strange with this *now;* no matter how hard you thought:
"Now," it passed. It was like long ago when he would
watch Saskia ride off on her bicycle on Monday morn-
ings, after having spent the weekend with him. She
would wave, mount her bike, wave again, and ride down
the street. He would press his cheek against the farthest
corner of the window and think, Now I can still see her.
And now, too. And even now! But no matter how hard

he thought this, it would not stop her, and even as he was thinking his last *now,* she'd have disappeared.

He drank. It was black coffee with sugar, hot and bitter.

He returned the cup. Lemorne looked into it, and then told him what had happened, from the moment that Saskia had asked for change until he drove away from the TOTAL station with her. Rex recognized her. Lemorne spoke slowly, never searching for a word, a sober tale without malice; *he* had done this, *she* had done that, *this* was what had come of it.

The story was over, but the soporific had still not taken effect. Rex thought of something, and turning around he counted the fence posts. Crouching down near the eighth one, he removed the pebble lying against the cement base. By the dim light from the station and the highway he saw the soft double glint of the two coins.

He put the pebble back.

Returning to the little hill he sat down and looked at the letters TOTAL, now dark, above the gas station, and waited to fall asleep.

Lemorne waited too—the way a civilized person waits for a bus to arrive.

Rex dreamed he was sitting in a restaurant. Across from him was Saskia. He did not know her, but somehow he knew it was her. Everything was about to begin. The restaurant was all gray inside, dimly lit. She hadn't ordered anything, but he was served a plate full of tennis balls. When he cut one open a duck emerged, spread its wings, and flew away.

Rex woke up.

He opened his eyes, but it made no difference: He saw only black.

He felt he was alone. He gasped for air: So this was it, this was what had happened to Saskia. Where *was* he?

He lay in the blackness, unable to fasten his fear onto anything. He sat up, but knocked his forehead and fell back. He landed on something soft and felt along his body with his hands: He lay on a mattress, a single mattress; the edges of it were right next to him.

There was no sound, the air was heavy and cold.

There was a wall to his left along the mattress. He wanted to touch his head to see how badly he had knocked it, but as he did so his knuckles hit something directly above him. He reached up—it was not a beam that he had touched, but a kind of wooden ceiling, not more than two hands' width above his face.

Now he knew. It was too awful to know.

Cautiously, to postpone the certainty, he felt to his right. There, too, was a wooden wall. Behind his head was a partition, and another one below his feet. He pounded his fists above his head and to his sides and screamed, but heard nothing, as if the sound were swallowed by the darkness.

Gaaahd!

He lay in a coffin, buried alive.

That this should have happened to Saskia! That she had been lying here like this, begging him to come to her rescue, yet knowing he never *could* come . . .

The loneliness of this!

Keep calm, he thought, but a limitless panic spread through his veins, faster than his blood. Keep calm, do something to calm down. But the thought that whatever would be calm would be grievously locked up here made him mad with fear. The walls held him in their grip, without hope.

How long had he been lying here? A month? Suppose I cannot even die? thought Rex, and he burst out sobbing.

Later he noticed that his fear was fighting him and using *his* body.

Stay calm, he thought. I've been lying here fifteen minutes. My name is Rex Hofman. When he thought how absurd it was to have a name in a place like this, he began to laugh.

5

When Lieneke received Rex's letter she was busy giving her room its monthly cleaning. She put the letter on her table and continued cleaning until the job was finished. For the first time in ages she emptied the entire dish rack, rewashed some of the plates, wiped them dry, and put everything away in the cabinet.

Then she sat down and read the letter. She read it five times in a row. Immature whining, she thought. I love him. But I'll never be able to take him away from Saskia.

She had no idea how to react. She called a good friend who was also an acquaintance of Rex's, and he advised her to run into him accidentally. The letter had arrived on a Saturday, so she decided to wait until the following weekend. All week long she left the phone off the hook whenever she had to go out.

Friday and Saturday she went to some cafés where he might be but he wasn't there. He did not phone either. On Sunday she called him but there was no answer. On

Monday she called every fifteen minutes, all day long, with the same result. She bicycled over to his flat, where his car stood stupidly staring at her.

Finally she took the bull by the horns and rang his doorbell, but no one answered. She went home and called his parents, who were surprised, then the editor of his magazine, where they had been waiting in vain for his article on Cantor, and then the police.

A few days later Rex's picture was in the paper. Some witnesses called in, among them the woman who had left his apartment that Friday morning and who appeared to be the last person to have seen him. She had found him rather absent.

Rex Hofman had vanished without a trace. The fact that he had been in the midst of an expensive advertising campaign in French newspapers to find his girlfriend Saskia Ehlvest, who had disappeared eight years earlier, attracted attention. For some time thereafter the portraits of Rex and Saskia were shown together on television, and in newspapers and magazines.

This turned up nothing, nor did a new investigation at the *Venoy-Grosse-Pierre* TOTAL station. And in all of the 145 letters from France that finally arrived in Rex's post office box, there was nothing that could shed any light on his disappearance or that of Saskia.

Nothing was ever heard of either of them again—they seemed to have vanished from the face of the earth.